DREAMS IN INK
Tales for kids

GAURI SINGHAL

BLUEROSE PUBLISHERS
India | U.K.

Copyright © Gauri Singhal 2024

All rights reserved by author. No part of this publication may be reproduced, stored in a retrieval system or transmitted in any form or by any means, electronic, mechanical, photocopying, recording or otherwise, without the prior permission of the author. Although every precaution has been taken to verify the accuracy of the information contained herein, the publisher assume no responsibility for any errors or omissions. No liability is assumed for damages that may result from the use of information contained within.

BlueRose Publishers takes no responsibility for any damages, losses, or liabilities that may arise from the use or misuse of the information, products, or services provided in this publication.

For permissions requests or inquiries regarding this publication, please contact:

BLUEROSE PUBLISHERS
www.BlueRoseONE.com
info@bluerosepublishers.com
+91 8882 898 898
+4407342408967

ISBN: 978-93-6261-058-4

First Edition: August 2024

Dedicated to
My Most Beloved Nani

"My grandmother taught me everything, except how to live without her"

FOREWORD

TO OUR LITTLE ONE

Gauri, you are the little girl we always wished for and as we realize that you are more than halfway into being an adult, we want to tell you that you are definitely more than what we wished for. Raising you has been an absolute joy.

My dearest daughter, you are the sunshine of our lives and we can't tell how much we have enjoyed reading stories written by you. This is a small token of love we could think of gifting you which you can cherish forever.

Your boundless curiosity, infectious laughter and the twinkle in your eyes filled with imagination and creativity make this book a truly special one. Your endless enthusiasm for bedtime stories and the countless adventures you've shared are woven into the fabric of these pages.

May the magic within these pages continue to spark your imagination and nurture your love for stories. Stay fabulous, Stay delightful! Happy 11!

Your Beloved Parents

ACKNOWLEDGMENTS

We would like to extend our heartfelt gratitude to everyone who has contributed to the creation of this book of short stories by Gauri.

To God and Gauri's grandparents for all the blessings and love.

To Gauri herself, for her creativity, imagination, and dedication in bringing these stories to life.

To her friends, her Uncle and family, for their unwavering support and encouragement throughout this journey.

To her school and teachers for all the guidance and motivation.

Last but not the least, to her Asha Didi and little brother Amogha for showering their unconditional love at all times.

And to all the readers, for taking the time to embark on this literary adventure with us. Your appreciation and feedback mean the world to us. Thank you for being a part of this wonderful journey.

INTRODUCTION

"Dreams in Ink: Tales for Kids" is a delightful collection of short stories penned by an imaginative 11-year-old girl. Each story invites readers into a world of wonder, where magic and reality intertwine, where dreams take flight, and where the imagination knows no bounds.

In "The Secret Experiment", readers are introduced to five young scientists who take over a secret government project and impress the smart Chairman with their skills. In "The Case of Missing Treasure", a young detective embarks on a quest to uncover the culprit behind a disappearing treasure, leading to an unexpected twist that will keep readers guessing until the very end. In "An Adventurous Picnic", readers accompany a curious adventurer as she stumbles upon a secret place that leads to a fantastical realm filled with toys and cookies. In "At dinner table in my dreams", author is wishful with God to meet three personalities who are ideal to her.

From heartwarming tales of friendship and adventure to whimsical fantasies filled with talking alien and beautiful fairies, this collection showcases the boundless creativity and imagination of this young author. With each story, readers are invited to embark on a journey of discovery, where dreams come to life and the impossible becomes possible.

"Dreams in Ink: Tales for Kids" is a testament to the magic of storytelling and the joy of seeing the world through the eyes of a young dreamer. Filled with charm, humor, and heart, this enchanting collection of short stories is sure to captivate readers of all ages and inspire them to embrace their own creativity and imagination.

Join the adventure and let your dreams take flight within the pages of this charming book.

TABLE OF CONTENTS

THE LOST TEDDY 1

THE SECRET EXPERIMENT 3

AT THE DINNER TABLE IN MY DREAMS 7

AN ADVENTUROUS PICNIC 10

THE SOFT PILLOW 14

THE BANGING DOOR 16

MONSTER AT MY BIRTHDAY PARTY 20

TRIP TO THE MOON 28

THE CASE OF MISSING TREASURE 31

MYSTERIOUS NIGHT 36

THE LOST TEDDY

Once upon a time, there lived a girl "Ria". She loved to play with teddies. On 5th birthday, her parents took her to the fair. Ria wanted to take her teddy too and her parents agreed. When they arrived at the fair, Ria ran towards merry-go-round, hopped on the horse and went round and round.

As she came down, she didn't find her teddy. Looking at her sad face, her mother said, "Don't worry Ria, somebody will find your teddy and give it to us". Unhappy Ria took hold of her father's hand and started walking towards the

car. As she sat down in the car, she heard someone shouting – "Ria, look what I found!". She turned back and saw her friend "Priya" coming towards her with her teddy. She shouted with joy and they both started dancing. She thanked Priya and said sorry to her parents. Ria's parents bought **balloons** for them and asked her to be careful from next time. They all lived happily ever.

THE SECRET EXPERIMENT

It was a bright sunny day. I was sitting in my classroom. Just then our class teacher came in. We wished her a good morning. She had a very important announcement to make. She told us that a high-level committee is coming to our school to select a group of students for a secret government experiment. I was on cloud nine.

Later that day, me and four other fellow students were called in the Coordinator's office. We all got scared and nervous. Coordinator Mam told that we are selected for the secret experiment. She also told us that we'll go to Delhi for a week to conduct the experiment. All five of us were very happy.

The next day we went to Delhi and met the chairman. He addressed us that it is a top-secret experiment and should not be told to anyone. He also told us one thing we never knew. We would design a gadget which is supposed to give us superpowers to become invisible. It was basically planned to help the Indian **Army** fight in extremely difficult situations. We all were scared but excited too. In the process we faced many difficulties but didn't give up. Every day we were given different tasks to complete. We used to complete them quite successfully. We all were eagerly waiting for the final outcome. But soon we learnt that the experiment was more dangerous than we thought because another feature of the gadget was that we would be visible in red light.

So, if during the war the enemy has a red colored light and somehow the secret is revealed, he would move it around and if he sees us, we would be caught and killed. We were also afraid of this feature but the chairman perhaps read our minds. He called all of us and explained the importance of the experiment. He convinced us by saying that it was just an experiment and he will take care of all the safety issues. At the end of the week, we were ready with the final outcome. The chairman was very happy and appreciated our efforts. We returned to our school happily. It was a **memorable** experience, indeed.

AT THE DINNER TABLE IN MY DREAMS

If I were to invite three famous people for a meal, I would invite

1. VIKRAM BATRA

The superhero of Kargil war and my inspiration. I have seen the movie 'Shershah' but I want to hear about all his experiences and events during the war. He is the ideal person I look at as I grow up and wish to become a **soldier**. At the dinner table, I want to gift my painting to him as a token of love and respect.

2. SUNDAR PICHAI

I would like to give thanks to him for creating Google where I can search almost everything and for Gmail from which I can send an email to my **friends**. While having tasty food during dinner, I will ask him to make a special platform for kids by which I can search, email, call, paint, do online classes and watch cartoons.

3. MY GRANDFATHER

who passed away long back before I was born. That would be a very happy day when I can actually see him and talk to him. Whenever I gaze at the sky on a starry night, I find my Baba- the shining star, looking at me with all his love and blessings

AN ADVENTUROUS PICNIC

One day, my school arranged a **picnic** to Mussourie for grade 5. Children were very happy. Me and my friends were also excited and singing songs. Suddenly, a big stone fell on the road and bus stopped. The driver said, "It will take some time before we can go ahead".

We walked down to explore the beauty of nature. As I moved few steps, I heard a voice and it was my **friend** asking to explore a secret passageway. "We have no idea where it is going", I said. "Let's **walk** around and discover", she answered.

We entered into a big house where the first room was the living room. It was very dirty with spider webs all around. On the other side was the kitchen and dining area. In a corner, there was a note pasted on the wall showing an arrow sign towards the stairs. Both of us were curious and walked up to find a library.

On the table there was a code saying, "The book - TGSHEG SDGIAGSRGY SGOSF SAG GWIMGPYS GKIDS, Solve if you can, to find the secret place".

My friend and I tried to solve the code and found that on removing G's and S's, it's the name of a famous book "THE

DIARY OF A WIMPY KID". We ran to find the book in the shelves. Inside the book we found a note having a room number and the key number to unlock the SECRET PLACE. We both were afraid and excited at the same time to open the room. Holding each other hands, me and my friend opened the room and Wow!!! There was a sign board that said, "THE SECRET CHILDREN's PLACE". It was filled with lots of toys, books and candies. We stuffed our stomach with candies, packed our bag with **toys** and ran away without looking back. When we reached near our bus, we took a breath and told the entire story to our teacher.

The teacher promised to visit our secret place again soon.

THE SOFT PILLOW

Once upon a time, there lived a pretty girl named Emily. She liked soft pillows but she didn't have any. One day, she went to the market with her mother. She saw a pillow with shiny sequences. She liked the pillow and wanted to buy it. Emily said to her mother, "Mom, I want to buy that pillow". Her mother replied, "Ok, let's go and see how much does it cost". When they went to the shop they saw that it was very costly. Her mother said, "Sorry dear, we cannot buy it instead we can buy this canvas. You can well paint it. It's just that i don't have enough cash". Emily was sad. Her mother was very loving. Then, she saw her dog. It barked loudly. The dog moving his long tail, gave Emily's mother her wallet which she forgot at home. Her mother said, "My intelligent Entertainment! You remembered. Now I can buy this soft pillow for Emily".

THE BANGING DOOR

My exams were going on so I was studying till late night. I was thinking something when i heard banging of the door. It was quite loud. I tried to ignore it but it became louder and louder and was disturbing my **studies..** At first, I was scared but after few minutes, i went to my parents' bedroom to see if any one of them was awake. But they were sound asleep. Then I waited for sometime but the banging did not stop, instead became louder.

I was scared, worried but brave at the same time. So i decided to check. First, I had to figure out from where the noise was coming. It was coming from the rooftop. I climbed the stairs slowly as it was very dark. Though I could have switched on the lights but thought if it would be a thief, he would run away. I also took my phone with me to call the police, just in case. I tried to see who it was from the windows but couldn't see anything. I searched around myself for a torch.

When I found it, I looked outside the window and saw an UFO. It was very big in size. My mind was blown. Suddenly, a queer creature came in front of the window, just in a blink. I was terrified and fell on the floor. It was an alien. He waved and asked to come in. I was scared but then he started doing some funny moves and making funny noises which made me laugh, but still I was not sure, should I open the door or not. Then I asked him that was he a friendly one like I have seen in a movie. I also expected he would nod his head but to my great surprise he spoke English and said yes! I was stunned. I decided to call him Jaadu as it was just like a magic.

I played with him all night. We had lots of fun. As soon as it struck four, the alien sat in its UFO and vanished away in a fraction of seconds. Then i heard a voice saying "Wake up **Gauri**! You are getting late for school". Then i realized that i had slept on my study table while reading my EVS book. It was indeed a wonderful dream.

MONSTER AT MY BIRTHDAY PARTY

At my eleventh **birthday**, I had not invited many people, only my close friends. I had planned a sleepover for my friends the day before my birthday. As my birthday comes in summer season, we had planned to sleep on the terrace. I was really excited. The sleepover would begin at 9 PM but I had invited them at 8:30 PM so that we could collect some extra things from my house and have some extra fun.

Me and my parents had also set up an outdoor theater right under the night sky (which was ruined a million times by my little brother). We had put billions and billions of snacks and drinks in our homemade best-out-of-waste shelves. We had put a very **soft** and comfy sofa-cum-bed with a really soft thin blanket and many soft pillows too. We had put a really soft bedsheet on the cemented floor of the terrace and a huge LED TV on a solid shelf.

Everything there was very soft even the surface of the shelves and the border of the TV. Just a few meters away, was the sleeping area where all my friends' sleeping-bags would go forming a circular shape. In the middle would be a little space so that we could put toys, snacks or books. This area was also very soft. With the soft rug,, lots of cozy pillows – some with cute little pink hearts, some with **rainbow** in pastel colors and some with white cloud, all having smiling faces on them, this was my favourite section.

When my friends came, I was really busy collecting different things from all around my house and of course, as I knew where everything was, I just kept on giving my **friends** whatever I touched and running here and there. At last, when a few things were left, all my friends' hands were full, so I had to hold them. When we went upstairs, on the terrace, we realized that we had brought so much stuff that it was very difficult to fit all of it in the **shelves**. We had brought toys, food, books and many more things . As expected, it didn't fit there. So I came up with an incredible idea which everyone liked. I made shelves using all the story books we had brought.

While we were having fun upstairs, my parents had some scary prank going on in their mind downstairs. We all were supposed to be awake till 00:00 AM which was an *easy-peasy* task as we all were night owls. We had to be awake because the cake would be cut at midnight. Till then, we watched a movie which was really entertaining and also ate many snacks. All my friends liked it.

When it was 11:55 PM, a strong fast stroke of wind came from the west carrying a lot of dry leaves along with it . It also made a whistling sound. We all got scared and came close to each other. When it stopped, a black shadow appeared. We all gave a shriek but it was just my mother holding a birthday cake. We all took a sigh of relief. When I was about to cut the cake, I asked my mother, "Mumma! Where is Papa?" My mother looking confused too, replied – "I don't know darling. I haven't seen him either". We all started looking for him. Then I spoke up – "Well, it's okay. He might be downstairs…" "No, he isn't !" My mother exclaimed, "I just came checking".

Well, I guess, we should start cutting the birthday **cake**, I said. Everyone agreed. As we proceeded to cut the cake, another black shadow appeared. This time, we all were not quite scared. As we thought that it might be my father, so we didn't worry much. But when it came face to face, right in front of me, it was a ….can you guess ?? A big fat red-coloured monster !! We all got so scared that for a second, our jaws dropped and just the next second, we all were like 'Oggy and the Cockroaches'. All of us were running here and there like cockroaches and the monster was Oggy. We all were shouting and screaming terribly.

After a few minutes of running, I discovered that there was a zip at the back of the monster, and when I found the right moment, I pulled it down and the prank was revealed. It was my father! Right now, I was the only one who knew that it was my father so he took off his costume and told everyone that it was a prank. We all bursted with laughter. Then I cut the cake happily with everyone and we also cracked jokes. It was a really **funny** moment.

Then, we had the cake and tucked ourselves well in our sleeping bags. It really was the best and the most humorous night of my whole life. I will never forget it.

TRIP TO THE MOON

I always wondered that why the moon had so many spots on it. So to find out the reason behind it, once i went to the **moon** and met a **fairy**. Her skin was as

white as snow. Her lips were as red as blood. Her hair were yellow and as bright as the sun. She had a crown on her head with blue apatite stones on it. She had a magic wand with a blue crystal star on the top. She hugged me and it felt as if she was a deity. She moved her magic wand and gave me wings like hers. I was feeling as light as a feather. The fairy then took me to her house and to my great surprise, the whole house was made up of cheese! Different types of cheese were used to give colour to the house. I asked her if she could take me inside and give me a house tour. She nodded her head and we went inside. When she was giving the house tour, we kept on talking. I was seeing many fairies there so I asked her if they were her workers. She nodded her head again.

She told me that she was also known as the Cheese Fairy and she only made the moon cheesy that's why it has spots on it. I also saw pictures of rockets such as Apollo 11 and portraits of men such as Neil Armstrong. I was a little sleepy by now so she took me in the bedroom and sang a song in her melodious voice. Then I heard a voice - "Wake up Gauri! Time for School." When I opened my eyes, I saw that I was in my house and my mother was standing in front of me looking just like the fairy. Then I realized that it was just a dream.

THE CASE OF MISSING TREASURE

Hi! I'm **Gauri** and I am a detective. As I am a detective so of course, I love solving mysteries. Even when I was little, I loved solving **mysteries.** I used to ask my friend to hide a toy somewhere and become the thief and I used to be the detective.

Nowadays, my team and I are investigating a case of missing treasure. Someone has stolen a lot of coins from the Coin Collection at the Indian Museum, Kolkata. The staff of the museum is saying that some cleaning work was in process that day. They also said that they only have women staff for cleaning and that day all the women except eight were cleaning the **coins**. Later on, when the museum was closing and the staff had gone, they remembered that one woman from the cleaning staff said that she won't come because her child was very sick. If the woman really didn't come then one woman was extra.

They immediately called her through the phone and asked her if she really came. She said that she didn't. She was looking after her child all day. Now we are checking all the CCTVs footage, and we have just got a clue! One camera, which was outside the Coin Collection and was monitoring the road, captured a footage in which a woman was getting out of a car in the parking on the roadside, wearing the staff's uniform. She was getting inside the window. This footage was captured around 5:00 AM in the morning when the museum was not even open. Then another camera, which was inside, captured a footage in which the woman was looking for precious coins to steal. Then she hid behind one of the cupboards of coins and waited till the museum opened and the cleaning staff came to clean the coins.

Now, we are looking at the footage of the road again and writing down the number of the car. We have given the police the number of the car and the police is tracing the car. We are going to its exact location with the police. It is in the middle of a **village**. The next day, when we reached there, we found that she belonged to a gang of robbers who were stealing antiques from all over the country. Then they sell it to other countries. We took the woman and the other members of the gang to the police station and put her in prison. Hence, the missing treasure was found and the case was solved.

MYSTERIOUS NIGHT

Once, I went to my friend's house for a night stay. Her parents were to come back late at night and we were all alone. Suddenly, we heard funny noises from under our bunk bed.

I whispered into my friend's ear, "What is that?" She said "Is it a **monster**?" I resisted "Monsters are nothing." But she said "I am scared. Let's climb on the upper bed."

After some time, the funny noises stopped. We came down to see what it is. My friend said "You check because I am scared". I checked and saw her pet puppy Tommy playing with a trumpet and making funny noises. I told her "Look, it is not a monster. It is your pet Tommy."

After the mystery was solved, both of us laughed a lot. But suddenly, we heard doors opening. We both were scared. She asked "What is that?" to which I replied with fear "It is another mystery."

We went outside the room to check who is that. My friend said "Is it a ghost? I am scared." I said "Don't worry."

When we checked, we saw her parents. She told them whatever happened and we laughed a lot and had lots of fun. And from that day, we both loved to solve mysteries.

LIFE LESSONS FROM MY NANI

My Nani taught me a lot – about life, about love, about what it means to be a good person. She was giving, kind, compassionate. Even when she was at her sickest, she never faltered in her positivity and tenacious spirit. I wouldn't be the girl I am today if it wasn't for my grandma. Every decision I make, there is always this underlying question I ask myself, "Would this make my Nani proud?" She was always more than a Nani to me, but someone I considered a mentor and a friend.

1. Family first – always

My Nani was all about family – she was happiest rocking a baby, loved big family get-togethers and lavished all her attention on her grandchildren. I would spend countless entire weekends at her house and she was always so happy to have us there. Nani taught me the importance of family.

2. Most important relationship of life – God's Worship

My Nani was a devout Hindu and believed in God with her full heart. Her belief in Lord Shiva was inspirational. She taught me about the Ramayana, about Shiva, Krishna, Hanuman, and Ambe Gauri. She was the one who taught me to pray. I'm so grateful I was the recipient of her prayers for me for so many years, especially the ones I never heard.

3. Make people feel loved, appreciated, and special

Nani taught me that everyone is deserving of love and making people feel so is the best gifts you can give. She always made people feel good, accepted, loved, and cherished. Whenever I was around her, my spirits instantly lifted and I felt better about myself and my life.

4. Chocolate is a cure for almost everything

I thank my Nani for my raging sweet tooth. My fondest memories of that time were the nights spent with my grandma – drinking hot chocolate and eating something sweet, talking about life and reminiscing on the past. Nani taught me to love my guilty pleasures and to never apologize for them.

5. You are not your circumstances

One of the biggest lessons my Nani taught me was never be a victim. She never questioned why or blamed God or complained about anything. She left us due to a heart attack, but she was never a patient, in-fact. Nani taught me that I am not my anxiety, I am not my weight, I am not my singleness. I am Gauri – and that is perfectly enough.

www.ingramcontent.com/pod-product-compliance
Lightning Source LLC
LaVergne TN
LVHW061626070526
838199LV00070B/6601